This Book is from My
1st grade teacher.

I had her for 1st grade
+ 4th grade.

This book belongs to:
Diana Bellucci
Love,
Miss Mullen
1988
Christmas

Text Copyright © 1986 by Joshua Morris Pubishing Inc.
167 Old Post Road
Southport, Connecticut 06490

This 1986 edition published by Derrydale Books,
distributed by Crown Publishers, Inc.
225 Park Avenue South, New York, New York 10003

Printed in West Germany

h g f e d c b a

ISBN 0-517-62732-9

At Home with the Christmas Gnomes

Illustrated by Erik Forsman

Derrydale Books
New York

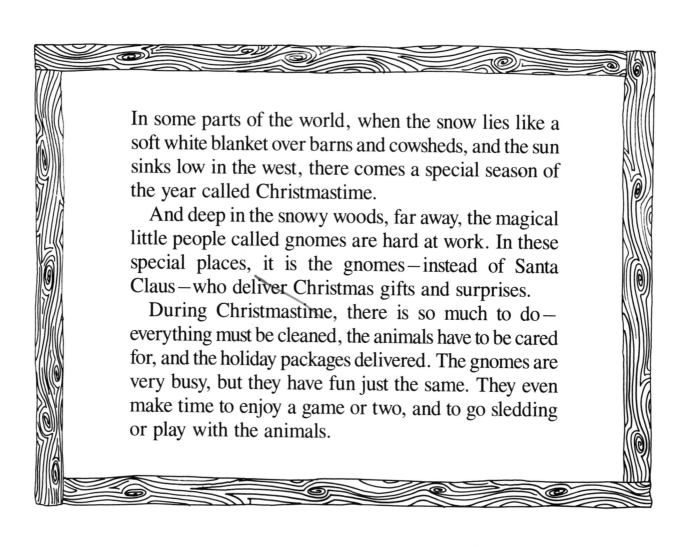

In some parts of the world, when the snow lies like a soft white blanket over barns and cowsheds, and the sun sinks low in the west, there comes a special season of the year called Christmastime.

And deep in the snowy woods, far away, the magical little people called gnomes are hard at work. In these special places, it is the gnomes—instead of Santa Claus—who deliver Christmas gifts and surprises.

During Christmastime, there is so much to do—everything must be cleaned, the animals have to be cared for, and the holiday packages delivered. The gnomes are very busy, but they have fun just the same. They even make time to enjoy a game or two, and to go sledding or play with the animals.

Everyone is busy up on Gnome Hill. The horses must be groomed and the sleds checked. There is wood to chop and the barn must be cleaned out. Just the same, some of the gnomes still find time to dance a merry jig.

Here you can see just how busy it is in the gnomes' workshop. The gnomes hide in a secret place deep under the stables where no human would ever look. Anything and everything happens here and the gnomes sing this little song while they work:

Drying out the damp gnome socks,
Packing presents in a box.
Boiling soup and making sauce.
And baking Christmas cakes of course!
Painting, drawing, making toys —
For all the little girls and boys.
Writing verses that should rhyme.
What a busy, happy time!

Christmas baking is a must! All year long, the gnomes collect flour for their Christmas treats. You'd be amazed at how much flour and sugar people spill—and if a mouse gnaws a hole in a flour sack, the gnomes sweep up the spilled flour and patch the sack as best they can. It is quite a task, you know!

Many of the presents have to be carried a long, long way, so the gnomes load up the sleigh, harness the horse, and give him a taste of Christmas cake. After all, it is Christmas for the animals, too, not just for people and gnomes!

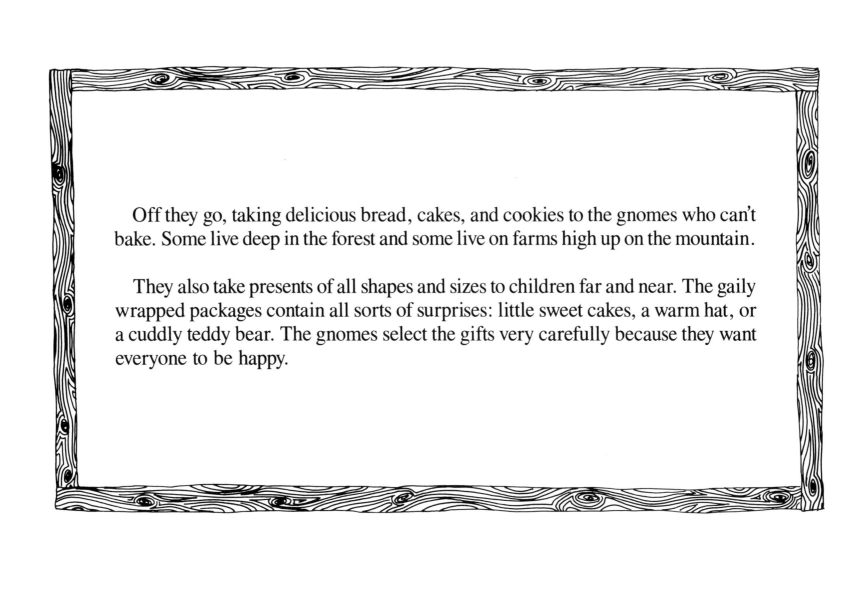

Off they go, taking delicious bread, cakes, and cookies to the gnomes who can't bake. Some live deep in the forest and some live on farms high up on the mountain.

They also take presents of all shapes and sizes to children far and near. The gaily wrapped packages contain all sorts of surprises: little sweet cakes, a warm hat, or a cuddly teddy bear. The gnomes select the gifts very carefully because they want everyone to be happy.

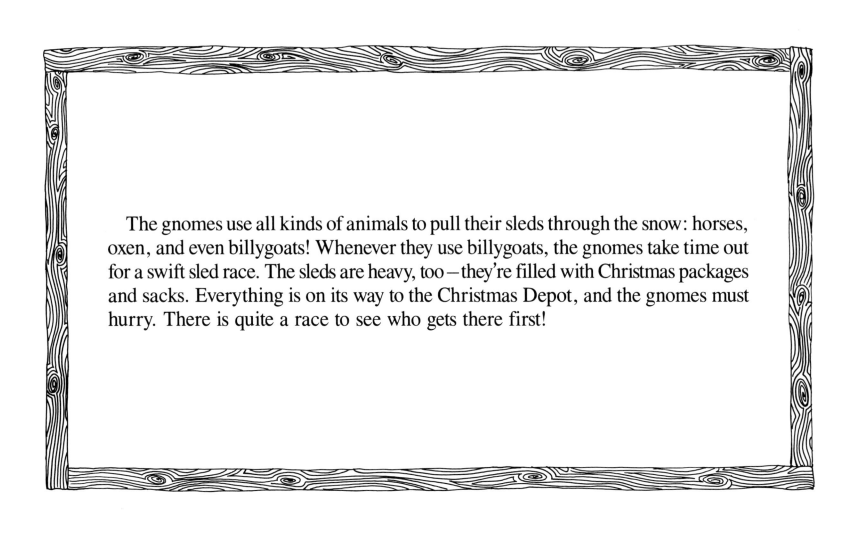

The gnomes use all kinds of animals to pull their sleds through the snow: horses, oxen, and even billygoats! Whenever they use billygoats, the gnomes take time out for a swift sled race. The sleds are heavy, too—they're filled with Christmas packages and sacks. Everything is on its way to the Christmas Depot, and the gnomes must hurry. There is quite a race to see who gets there first!

The Christmas Depot is a very secret place which humans will never find, no matter how hard they may try. You might try sometime, but be careful that you don't get lost! If you come across a place where you find many animal tracks, then it *might* be a place where the gnomes have gathered! There is usually a cave nearby where they can shelter if the weather is bad. The gnomes gather from far and wide and cook porridge for themselves and the animals who pass by. Animals love gnome-porridge. In fact, they like gnome-porridge just as much as the gnomes like the porridge that humans make! (But that is a secret, so please don't tell anyone!)

The gnomes make the porridge in a huge bucket and the bucket stands good and firm down among the rocks. It's the best porridge in the world! It's so good, in fact, that the hungry gnomes can hardly wait till it's ready. This is when they exchange their presents, so they have something to do while the porridge is cooking.

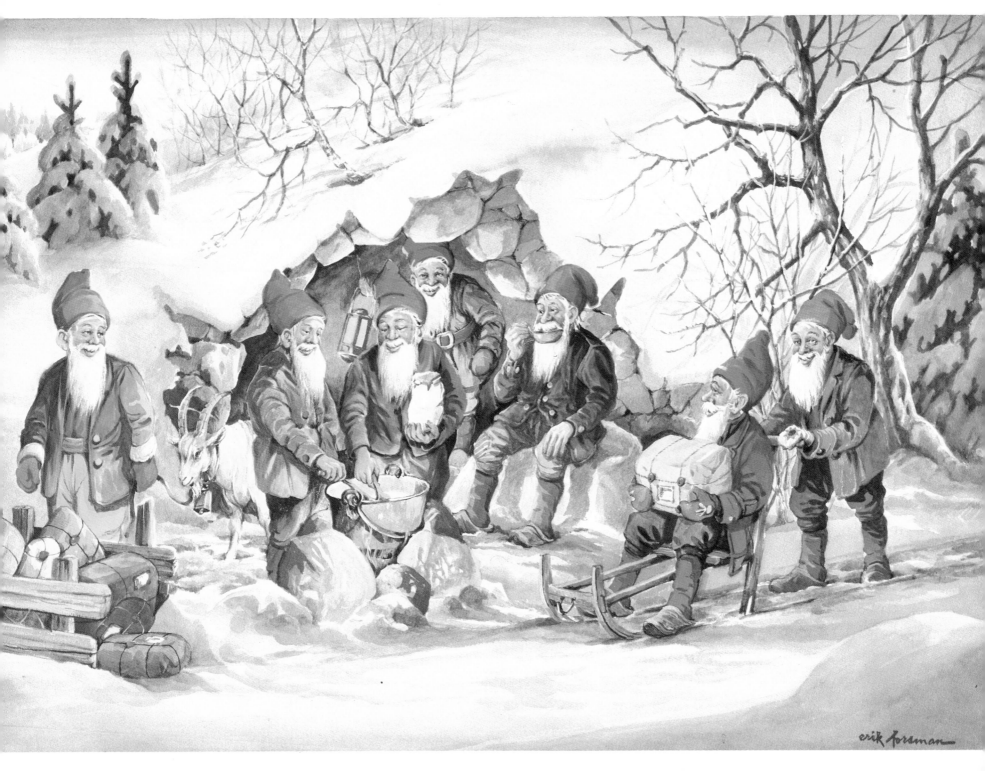

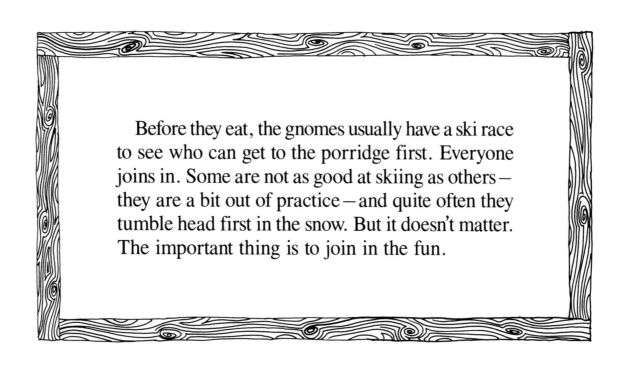

Before they eat, the gnomes usually have a ski race to see who can get to the porridge first. Everyone joins in. Some are not as good at skiing as others — they are a bit out of practice — and quite often they tumble head first in the snow. But it doesn't matter. The important thing is to join in the fun.

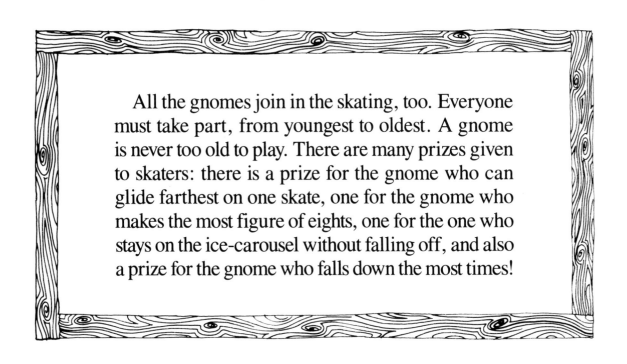

All the gnomes join in the skating, too. Everyone must take part, from youngest to oldest. A gnome is never too old to play. There are many prizes given to skaters: there is a prize for the gnome who can glide farthest on one skate, one for the gnome who makes the most figure of eights, one for the one who stays on the ice-carousel without falling off, and also a prize for the gnome who falls down the most times!

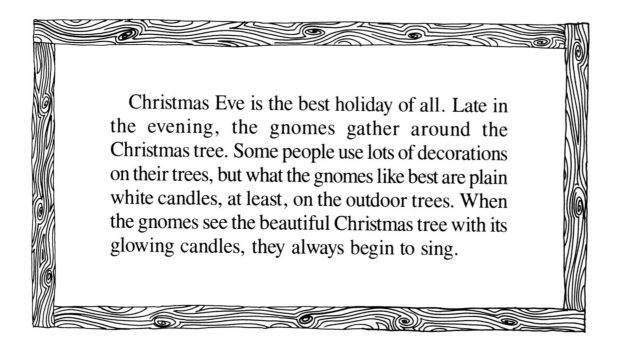

Christmas Eve is the best holiday of all. Late in the evening, the gnomes gather around the Christmas tree. Some people use lots of decorations on their trees, but what the gnomes like best are plain white candles, at least, on the outdoor trees. When the gnomes see the beautiful Christmas tree with its glowing candles, they always begin to sing.

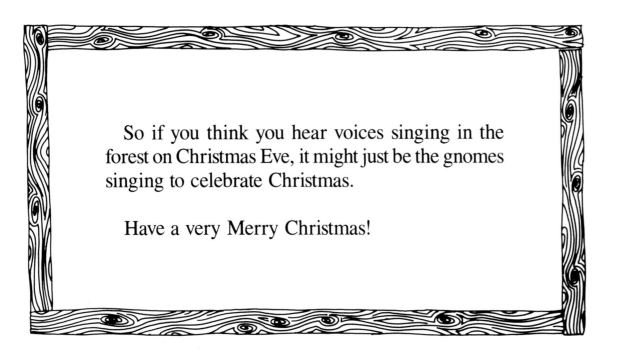

So if you think you hear voices singing in the forest on Christmas Eve, it might just be the gnomes singing to celebrate Christmas.

Have a very Merry Christmas!